Katja Spitzer

Where's Bernard?

A Bat Spotting Book

Prestel

Munich · London · New York

This is Bernard. It's his birthday today and he would like
to spend this special night with all of his friends.

He's going to need a few things for his big party. What can they be?
Just take a peek at the right-hand page.

Can you help Bernard with his search?
In each of the following pictures, try to spot one of these party objects — as well as Bernard himself!

Balloons

Cocoa Pot

Magical Hat

Guitar

Birthday Cake

Message in a Bottle

Crystal Star

Garland

Juggling Balls

Even the octopus is feeling good in this greenhouse! There must surely be a magical hat hidden away somewhere. The magician is going to need it. Can you find the hat for Bernard?

Thousands of sparkling crystals lie beneath the earth in this cavern.
Can you discover the crystal star? Let's hope it fits into Bernard's backpack!

A birthday party would not be the same
without music. Bernard wants to borrow a guitar
from a friend in the village.
But where is it?

Sina the beetle has some colorful balloons for the party. Bernard wants to meet her at the ice rink. Wow, it's really cold here — and slippery! But where has Sina hidden the balloons?

Bernard has arrived in the garden of lovely flowers.
He wants to pick up his cocoa pot from the gardeners.
Do you see how they are using the pot?

There's a lot going on in the woods at nighttime.
How on earth can Bernard find the colorful garland for his party?
Can you help him?

There's a message in a bottle for Bernard!
Sadly, it has sunk deep down into the water.
Will you dive with Bernard to the bottom
of the sea and find it?

The only thing we need to get now are
six juggling balls. Bernard has left them with
his family. Before gathering them up, he has a nice cup of hot cocoa.
Maybe you can spot all the juggling balls before he does?

Happy Birthday Bernard! All of his friends have arrived to celebrate with him. You've already met Bernard's friends, but can you remember where?

Bernard's birthday party goes on throughout the whole night. But that's not such a bad thing. Bats love nighttime, and they sleep all day anyway.

© 2017, Prestel Verlag, Munich · London · New York
A member of Verlagsgruppe Random House GmbH
Neumarkter Strasse 28 · 81673 Munich

Prestel Publishing Ltd.
14–17 Wells Street
London W1T 3PD

Prestel Publishing
900 Broadway, Suite 603
New York, NY 10003

Library of Congress Control Number: 2017932508
A CIP catalogue record for this book is available from the British Library.

Translated by: Paul Kelly
Copyedited by: Brad Finger
Project Management: Doris Kutschbach, Melanie Schöni
Design and Layout: Meike Sellier
Production management: Corinna Pickart
Separations: Reproline Mediateam, Munich
Printing und Binding: DZS Grafik, d.o.o., Ljubljana
Paper: Profimatt

Verlagsgruppe Random House FSC® N001967
Printed in Slowenia
ISBN 978-3-7913-7289-1
www.prestel.com